Miss Kittey

Sheriff

LITTLE DOGS
ON THE PRAIRIE

Gilroy

Patterson

To

From

Published in Nashville, Tennessee, by Tommy Nelson®, a division of Thomas Nelson, Inc.

Library of Congress Cataloging-in-Publication Data

Lollar, Phil.
    Yippee ti-yay happy birthday / written by Phil Lollar ; illustrations by John Jordan.
        p. cm. -- (Little dogs on the prairie)
    Summary: Includes instructions for games and recipes as well as songs, riddles, and poems to celebrate birthdays with a Western and prairie dog theme.
    ISBN 0-8499-7648-0
    1.Children's parties--Juvenile literature. 2. Birthdays--Juvenile literature. [1. Games. 2. Birthdays. 3. Parties. 4. Cookery. 5. Prairie dogs. 6. West (U.S.)] I. Jordan, John, 1953- ill. II. Title.

GV1205 .L65 2000
793.2'1 --dc21

                                                            00-032459

Printed in the United States of America

00 01 02 03 04 PHX 9 8 7 6 5 4 3 2 1

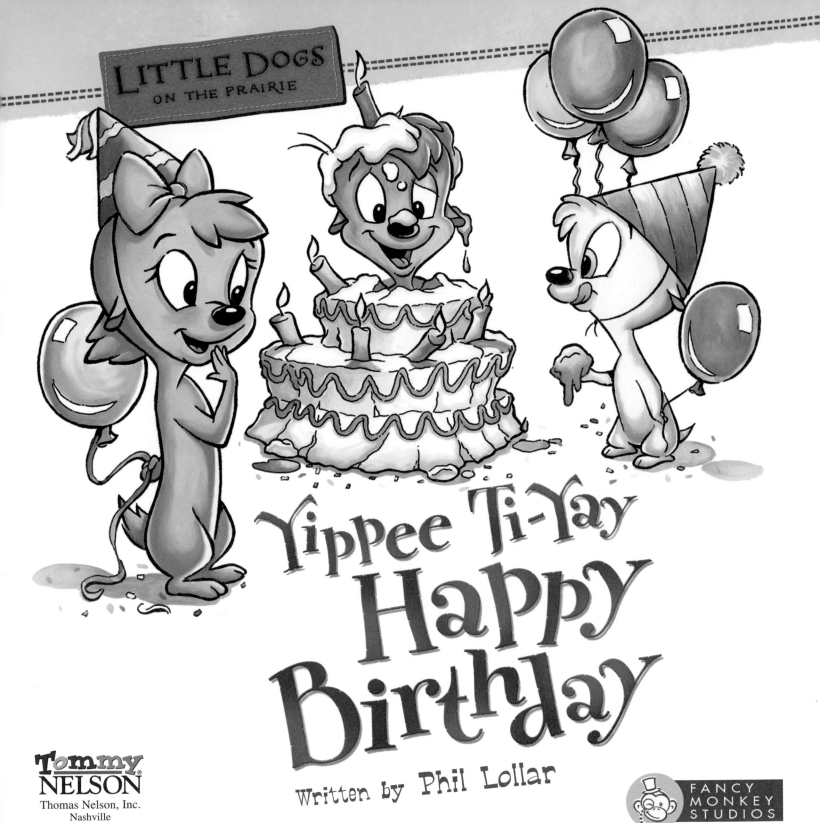

Little Dogs ON THE PRAIRIE

Yippee Ti-Yay Happy Birthday

Written by Phil Lollar

Tommy NELSON
Thomas Nelson, Inc.
Nashville

FANCY MONKEY STUDIOS

Whose Birthday Is It,

Scout was excited *and* confused.

He had just gotten a birthday invitation in the mail. Scout loved birthday parties! That's why he was excited.

But the invitation didn't say who was having a birthday party. It was just some squiggly lines. That's why he was confused.

Who could have sent it? Scout thought long and hard. It must have been Sport! His friend often played silly jokes on him.

"Are you playing a joke?" Scout asked Sport. But to Scout's surprise, Sport also had an invitation with only squiggly lines.

"Maybe it's Darcy!" said Sport.

Anyway?

eeTi-Yay

Yipp

to

They scampered to Darcy's house. But she had a strange-looking invitation, too!

"I thought you guys did this," she said.

"Not us," said Scout and Sport. "Maybe it was Miss Kitty!"

But Miss Kitty also had an invitation. And so did Hollister, Gilroy, Patterson, and Sheriff! Each invitation had squiggly lines on it, and each one invited a prairie dog to a wonderful birthday celebration.

But whose birthday celebration?

irthday

Darcy, Scout, Sport, the other prairie dogs, and Miss Kitty put their heads together—well, actually, they put their invitations together—to figure out the answer to the mystery. Can you figure it out? Do you know who is having a birthday?

Happ

B

y

You!

But our very biggest wish that we hope will come true

Help them find the way!

End

There's a Hole in the Old Prairie

(Sing to the tune of "There's a Hole in the Bottom of the Sea.")

There's a HOLE in the old prairie.
There's a HOLE in the old prairie.
There's a HOLE; there's a HOLE;
There's a HOLE in the old prairie.

There's a PARTY in the HOLE in the old prairie.
There's a PARTY in the HOLE in the old prairie.
There's a HOLE; there's a HOLE;
There's a HOLE in the old prairie.

The Little DOGS are at the PARTY in the HOLE in the old prairie.
The Little DOGS are at the PARTY in the HOLE in the old prairie.

There's a HOLE; there's a HOLE;
There's a HOLE in the old prairie.

There's a CAKE with the DOGS at the PARTY in the HOLE in the old prairie.
There's a CAKE with the DOGS at the party in the HOLE in the old prairie.
There's a HOLE; there's a HOLE;
There's a HOLE in the old prairie.

There's ICING on the CAKE with the DOGS at the PARTY in the HOLE in the old prairie.
There's ICING on the CAKE with the DOGS at the PARTY in the HOLE in the old prairie.
There's a HOLE; there's a HOLE;
There's a HOLE in the old prairie.

There're LETTERS in the ICING on the CAKE with the DOGS at the PARTY in the HOLE in the old prairie.

There're LETTERS in the ICING on the CAKE with the DOGS at the PARTY in the HOLE in the old prairie.

There's a HOLE; there's a HOLE;
There's a HOLE in the old prairie.

There're WORDS from the LETTERS in the ICING on the CAKE with the DOGS at the PARTY in the HOLE in the old prairie.

There're WORDS from the LETTERS in the ICING on the CAKE with the DOGS

at the PARTY in the HOLE in the old prairie.

There's a HOLE; there's a HOLE;
There's a HOLE in the old prairie.

The WORDS, they say, "HAVE A HAPPY BIRTHDAY!" using LETTERS in the ICING on the CAKE with the DOGS at the PARTY in the HOLE in the old prairie.

The WORDS, they say, "HAVE A HAPPY BIRTHDAY!" using LETTERS in the ICING on the CAKE with the DOGS at the PARTY in the HOLE in the old prairie.

There's a HOLE; there's a HOLE;
There's a HOLE in the old prairie.

Dog, Dog, Snake!

Here are two birthday games that Little Prairie Dogs love to play. You can play them with all of your friends, too! If you have a large room, these can both be inside games; otherwise, it is best to play them outside.

1. Everyone sits in a circle.

2. One person is It.

3. It walks around the outside of the circle gently tapping each person on the head and saying, "Dog."

4. At some point, It gently taps someone in the circle on the head and says, "Snake!"

5. It must run around the circle and sit in Snake's spot before Snake tags It.

6. If Snake catches It, then the game starts again with the same It, but if It makes it to Snake's spot, the game starts again with Snake as It.

Try it! It's fun!

Cactus, Tumbleweed

1. One person stands at one end of the yard. That person is the Caller.

2. Everyone else stands in a straight line, shoulder to shoulder, facing the Caller, but across the yard.

3. The Caller turns his or her back to the others.

4. Then the Caller can say "Cactus" or "Tumbleweed."

If the Caller says "Tumbleweed," all of the others move toward the Caller as fast as they dare.

If the Caller says "Cactus," the others must stop and freeze in place.

Now, the others can choose to keep moving forward, but they'd better be careful! The Caller can turn around at any time during "Cactus." If the Caller catches someone moving, then that person must go back to the starting line.

5. The first person to tag the Caller wins! That person then becomes the new Caller, and the game begins again!

Riddles & Knock, Knock Jokes

1 Scout and Darcy went to Sport's birthday party this morning. They rode on a blue stagecoach with green wheels. At the first stop, two prairie dogs got off, and three prairie dogs got on. At the second stop, one dog got off, and four dogs got on. At the third stop, six bison tried to get on, but they didn't have exact change. No dogs got off. At the fourth stop, Scout and Darcy got off. Here's the question: When was Sport's birthday party?

2 If you spell "most" M-O-S-T, and you spell "boast" B-O-A-S-T, and you spell "ghost" G-H-O-S-T, how do you spell what you put in a toaster?

3 Three prairie dogs passed by a table with a birthday cake cut into three slices. Each took one piece of cake, and that left two pieces of cake. How is this possible?

Knock, Knock.
Who's there?
Sheriff.
Sheriff who?
Sher, iff ya know
what's good
fer ya!

Knock, Knock.
Who's there?
Hollister.
Hollister who?
Holli, ster the
soup before
it boils over!

Knock, Knock.
Who's there?
Kittey.
Kittey who?
Kit tey-long little "doggie!"

ANSWERS:
1. This morning.
2. B-A-G-E-L. Or W-A-F-F-L-E. Oh, all right, B-R-E-A-D. ('Cause it's not toast when you put it in!)
3. One of the prairie dogs is named "Each." He's kind of strange. Doesn't hang around Others or Everyone.

D-A-R-C-Y, The Birthday Prairie Dog

(Sing to the tune of "B-I-N-G-O.") At each picture of clapping hands, clap your hands, too!

1) There is a birthday prairie dog with a twinkle in her eye   -y!

D- A- R- C- Y! D- A- R- C- Y! D- A-

R- C- Y! With a twinkle   in   her   eye   -y!

2) There is a birthday prairie dog, a girl and not a   guy   -y!

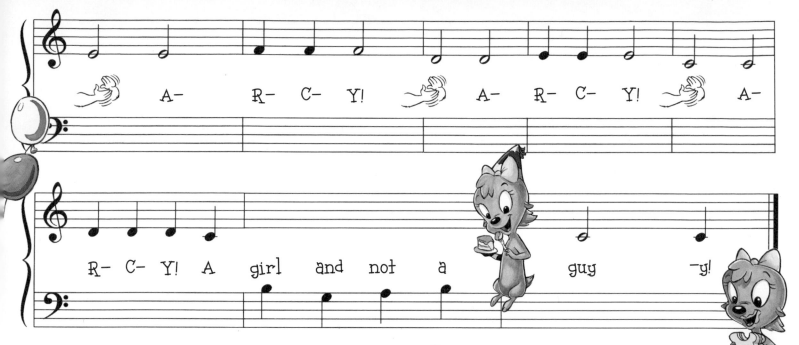

A- R- C- Y! A- R- C- Y! A-

R- C- Y! A girl and not a guy -y!

More Verses...

3) There is a birthday prairie dog
Who loves her cake and pie-ie!
🖐 - 🖐 -R-C-Y!
🖐 - 🖐 -R-C-Y!
🖐 - 🖐 -R-C-Y!

Who loves her cake and pie-ie!

4) There is a birthday prairie dog
Whose bow she loves to tie-ie!
🖐 - 🖐 - 🖐 -C-Y!
🖐 - 🖐 - 🖐 -C-Y!
🖐 - 🖐 - 🖐 -C-Y!

Whose bow she loves
to tie-ie!

5) There is a birthday
prairie dog
Who never wants
to lie-ie!
🖐 - 🖐 - 🖐 - 🖐 -Y!
🖐 - 🖐 - 🖐 - 🖐 -Y!
🖐 - 🖐 - 🖐 - 🖐 -Y!

Who never wants to
lie-ie!

6) There is a birthday prairie dog
Who likes corned beef on rye-y!
🖐 - 🖐 - 🖐 - 🖐 - 🖐 !
🖐 - 🖐 - 🖐 - 🖐 - 🖐 !
🖐 - 🖐 - 🖐 - 🖐 - 🖐 !

She likes corned beef
on rye-y!

7) If **you're** a birthday
prairie dog
Sing out and don't be shy-y!
H-A-P-P-Y!
H-A-P-P-Y!
H-A-P-P-Y!
B-I-R-T-H-D-A-Y!

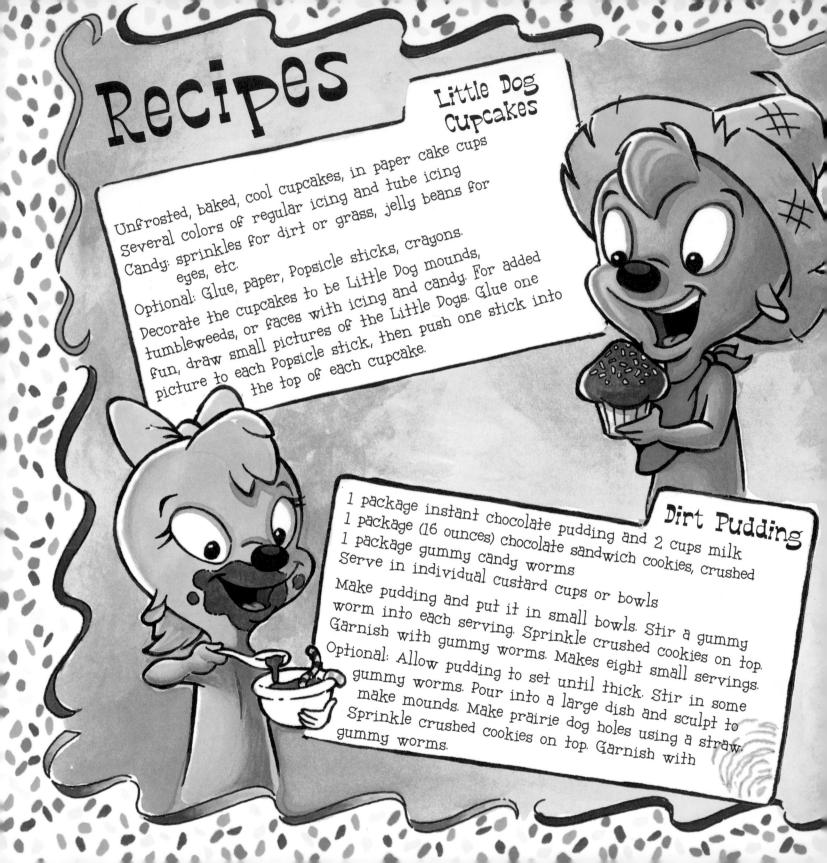

Recipes

Little Dog Cupcakes

Unfrosted, baked, cool cupcakes, in paper cake cups
Several colors of regular icing and tube icing
Candy: sprinkles for dirt or grass, jelly beans for
eyes, etc.

Optional: Glue, paper, Popsicle sticks, crayons.

Decorate the cupcakes to be Little Dog mounds,
tumbleweeds, or faces with icing and candy. For added
fun, draw small pictures of the Little Dogs. Glue one
picture to each Popsicle stick, then push one stick into
the top of each cupcake.

Dirt Pudding

1 package instant chocolate pudding and 2 cups milk
1 package (16 ounces) chocolate sandwich cookies, crushed
1 package gummy candy worms
Serve in individual custard cups or bowls

Make pudding and put it in small bowls. Stir a gummy
worm into each serving. Sprinkle crushed cookies on top.
Garnish with gummy worms. Makes eight small servings.
Optional: Allow pudding to set until thick. Stir in some
gummy worms. Pour into a large dish and sculpt to
make mounds. Make prairie dog holes using a straw.
Sprinkle crushed cookies on top. Garnish with
gummy worms.

These recipes combine three things the Little Dogs like to do: visit with each other, decorate, and eat! And you can share their fun with your friends, too. Here are some of their favorite recipes. . . . Remember, you'll need an adult helper for these projects.

Prairie Punch

2 quarts sweetened Kool-Aid (any flavor, but recommend tropical punch), chilled
1 quart unsweetened pineapple juice, chilled
2 quarts ginger ale, chilled
Optional: Float sliced oranges or lemons in punch.

Combine all ingredients in a glass or plastic container. (Do not store in a metal container.) Some of the punch can be frozen and placed in a punch bowl to keep punch chilled. Punch may also be served over ice. Makes 5 quarts.

Tumbleweed Popcorn Balls

1 cup brown sugar
1/2 cup margarine
30 large marshmallows
12 cups popped popcorn (about 1/2 cup corn)

In a large saucepan over medium heat, melt brown sugar, margarine, and marshmallows. Keep stirring it, so it won't burn. Once it's melted, pour evenly over all the popcorn. (It'll be HOT, so be careful on the following part. Don't want any scorched fingers.) Next, roll the popcorn into balls. Wrap each ball in plastic wrap. Let them cool and eat them up! Be sure you take the plastic off first, though. We've learned it's not nearly as good as the popcorn balls. Yield depends on size of popcorn balls.

Ode to Chocolate Cake

by Patterson

Today it was my birthday,
And it was such a treat!
'Cause we had lots
    And lots and lots
        Of chocolate cake to eat!

I also had a party,
Out yonder by the lake.
We rode a horse.
    And, oh, of course,
        We ate my chocolate cake.

We had presents and balloons.
And gifts with bows and laces.
Then by the lake
    With chocolate cake
        We all did stuff our faces.

I ate a piece. Then two. Then three.
Then onto number four.
I ate and ate,
    And ate and ate.
        And then I ate some more!

I simply opened up my mouth
And shoveled it all in.
I ate until

I had my fill—
    Then started in again!

Suddenly, I felt real odd.
Although the cake was yummy,
I felt a rum-tum-
    Rumbling
        Deep down inside my tummy

Ode to Birthday Balloons

by Gilroy

How could you do this to me
My lovely chocolate cake?
I'd had enough!
The lousy stuff
Gave me a stomach ache!

Today it was my birthday.
I turned six shades of green.
I'll ne'er partake
Of chocolate cake!
(Until next year, I mean!)

Birthday balloons
On days in June
Really make me happy.

Balloons of red
Balloons of white
All look really snappy.

I like to make things
Out of them.
I never want to stop.

I love balloons
I really do,
Except for when they pop.

Sheriff Says!

Ready for the next Prairie Dog birthday game? It also can be played inside or outside! And it's Sheriff's favorite!

1. Everyone stands in a straight line.

2. One person is Sheriff. Sheriff tells everyone else to do silly and fun things like "Stand on one foot," or "Pat your head with your left hand," or "Blink your eyes five times."

3. But here's the catch: Everyone else only follows the instructions if Sheriff starts them with "Sheriff says." For example, "Sheriff says, 'Stand on one foot.'"

4. Anyone who follows the instructions without Sheriff saying "Sheriff says" is OUT.

5. Anyone who does NOT follow the instructions when Sheriff says "Sheriff says" is OUT.

6. The last one out is the winner and becomes Sheriff.

Tongue Twister!

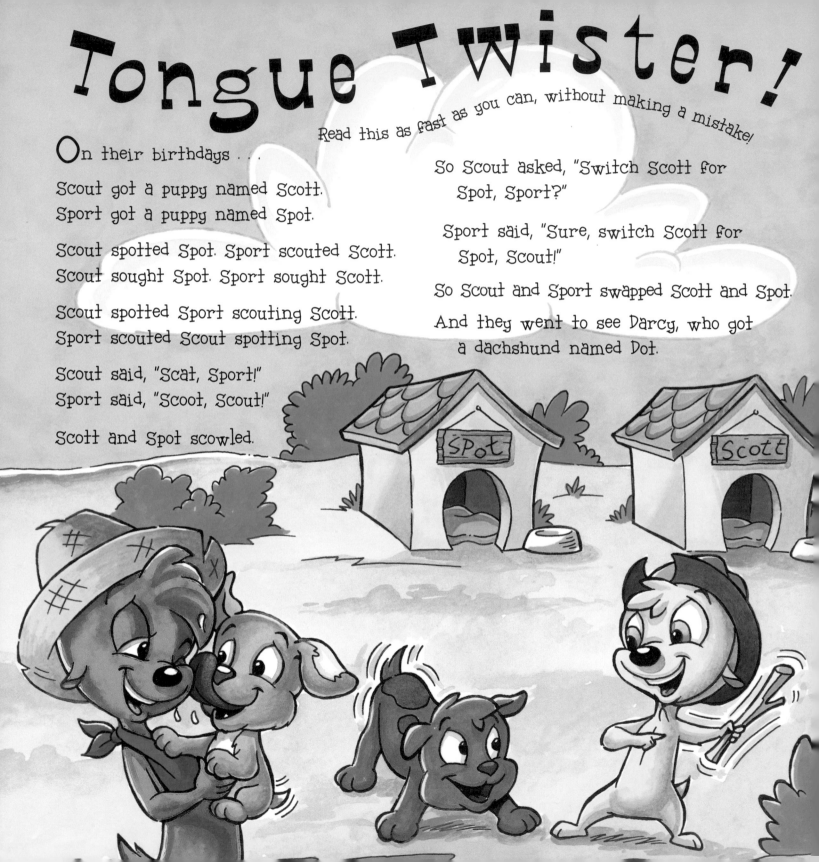

Read this as fast as you can, without making a mistake!

On their birthdays . . .

Scout got a puppy named Scott.
Sport got a puppy named Spot.

Scout spotted Spot. Sport scouted Scott.
Scout sought Spot. Sport sought Scott.

Scout spotted Sport scouting Scott.
Sport scouted Scout spotting Spot.

Scout said, "Scat, Sport!"
Sport said, "Scoot, Scout!"

Scott and Spot scowled.

So Scout asked, "Switch Scott for
Spot, Sport?"

Sport said, "Sure, switch Scott for
Spot, Scout!"

So Scout and Sport swapped Scott and Spot.

And they went to see Darcy, who got
a dachshund named Dot.

Rebus Story

A rebus story uses pictures and numbers for some words. Turn the page and read the story using the correct word from the dictionary below.

DICTIONARY

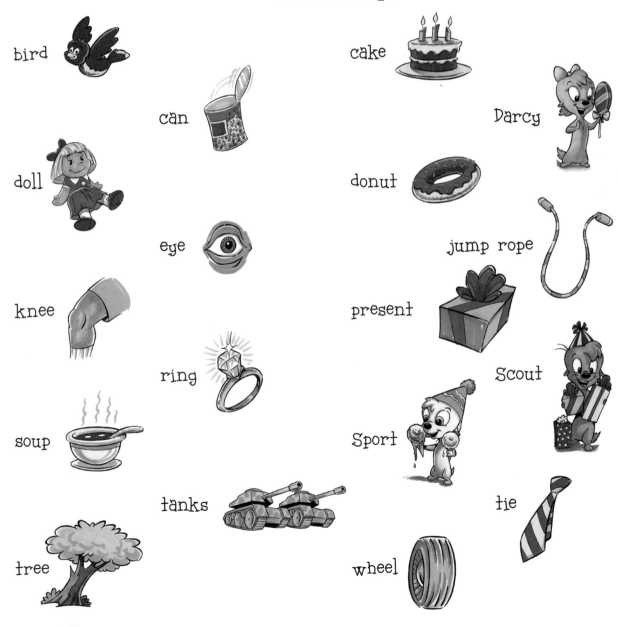

bird

can

doll

eye

knee

soup

tree

tanks

cake

Darcy

donut

jump rope

present

Scout

Sport

ring

tie

wheel

 's -A par-T

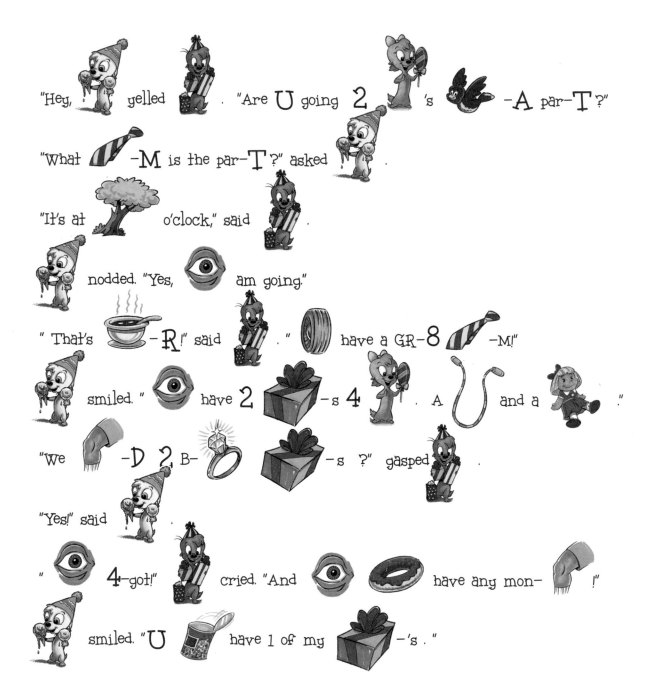

"Hey, yelled . "Are U going 2 's -A par-T?"

"What -M is the par-T?" asked .

"It's at o'clock," said .

nodded. "Yes, am going."

" That's -R!" said ." have a GR-8 -M!"

smiled. " have 2 -s 4 . A and a ."

"We -D 2 B- -s ?" gasped .

"Yes!" said .

" 4-got!" cried. "And have any mon- !"

smiled. "U have 1 of my -'s ."

!" said . "The ?"

"No!" said . "The !"

scowled. "If U say so."

" give the —'s 2 after we sing," said .

" sing?" asked .

nodded. "Yes. The "Hap-E -A" song!

"Do have 2 sing?" sneered .

"If U want the , U do," said .

S- -D. "Okay."

So they went 2 's par-T, 8 and cream,

sang the -A song, gave her the , -s and had a GR-8 -M!

Even if did have 2 give a .

Hope U have a GR-8 -A, 2!

Translation
Darcy's Birthday Party

"Hey, Sport!" yelled Scout. "Are you going to Darcy's birthday party?"

"What time is the party?" asked Sport.

"It's at Three o'clock," said Scout.

Sport nodded. "Yes, I am going."

"That's Super!" said Scout. "We'll have a great time!"

Sport smiled. "I have two presents for Darcy. A jump rope and a doll."

"We need to bring presents?" gasped Scout.

"Yes!" said Sport.

"I forgot!" Scout cried. "And I do not have any money!"

Sport smiled. "You can have one of my presents."

"Thanks!" said Scout. "The jump rope?"

"No!" said Sport. "The doll."

Scout scowled. "If you say so."

"We'll give the presents to Darcy after we sing," said Sport.

"We'll sing?" asked Scout.

Sport nodded. "Yes. The "Happy Birthday" song!

"Do I have to sing?" sneered Scout.

"If you want the present, you do," said Sport.

Scout sighed. "Okay."

So they went to Darcy's party, ate cake and ice cream, sang the birthday song, gave her the presents, and had a great time! Even if Scout did have to give Darcy a doll. Hope you have a great birthday, too!

Find the Hidden Pictures

The Little Dogs are on a birthday camping trip. Hidden in the camping scene are ten things you might find at a birthday party. Can you find the hidden pictures on the list?

A Cake ◉ 2 Balloons ◉ Bow ◉ Candle ◉ Ice-cream cone ◉ Invitation ◉
Noisemaker ◉ 2 Party hats ◉ Present ◉ Ribbon ◉

A Birthday Prayer

Dear Heavenly Father,

For my birthday, which is today,

For my friends who'll come to play,

For my cake with candles bright,

For my gifts, my bike and kite,

For my party with its favors,

For my ice cream's 31 flavors,

For my father and my mother,

Even for my mean old brother,

Blessings big and blessings small,

I thank You for them, one and all.

Help me, please, to not forget

To give this day, and not just get.

And thank You for Your Son who came.

All this I pray now, in His Name.

Amen.

Scout

Darcy

LITTLE DOGS
ON THE PRAIRIE

Sport

Hollister